This Little Tiger book belongs to:

For Scarlet who is just right to hug
and Beccy, her lovely mum ~ SS

For K, with love and hugs ~ CB

LITTLE TIGER PRESS
An imprint of Magi Publications
1 The Coda Centre, 189 Munster Road, London SW6 6AW
www.littletigerpress.com
First published in Great Britain 2010
This edition published 2011
Text copyright © Steve Smallman 2010
Illustrations copyright © Cee Biscoe 2010
Steve Smallman and Cee Biscoe have asserted their rights to be identified
as the author and illustrator of this work under the Copyright, Designs and Patents Act, 1988
A CIP catalogue record for this book is available from the British Library
All rights reserved • ISBN 978-1-84895-090-0 • Printed in China
LTP/1400/0144/0111
2 4 6 8 10 9 7 5 3 1

Too Hot to Hug!

Steve Smallman

Cee Biscoe

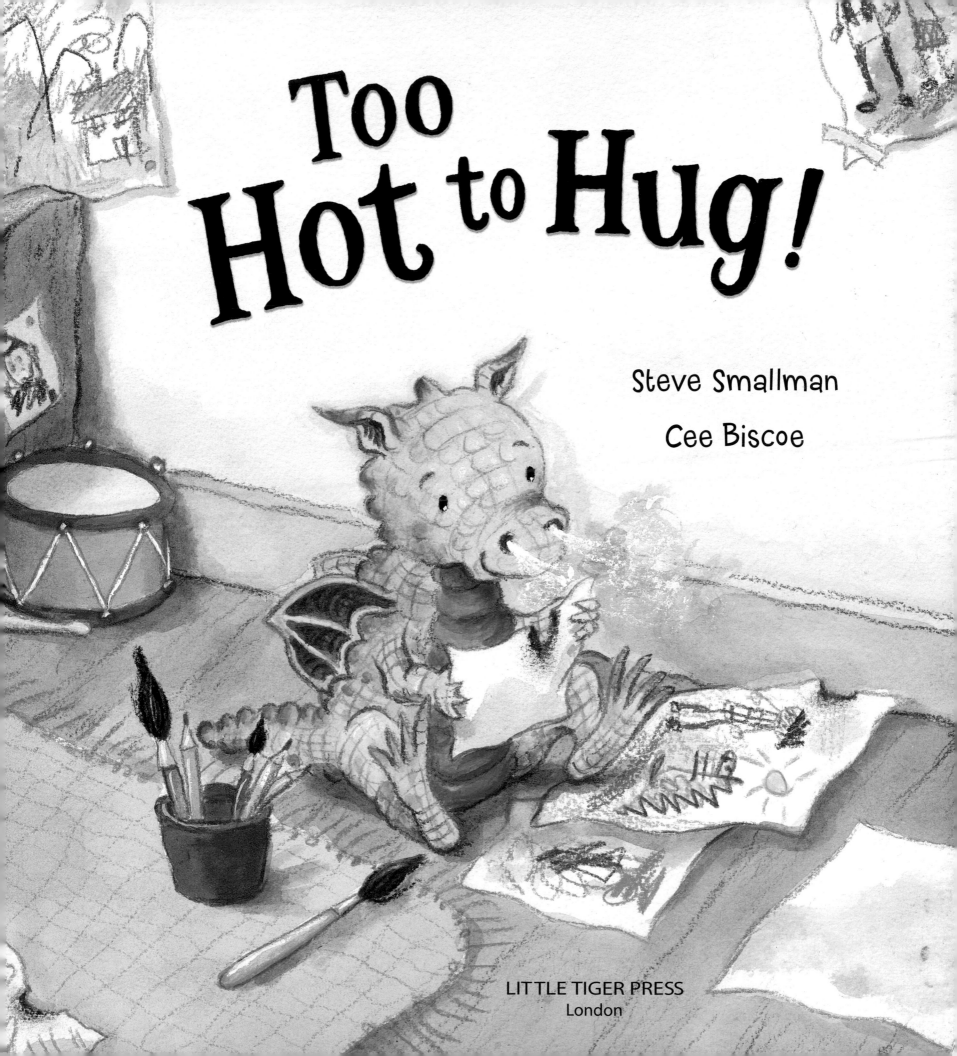

LITTLE TIGER PRESS
London

On the coldest day of a cold, cold winter, Rupert
was high in the mountains, searching for firewood.
His fingers were blue.
His nose was purple.
And he still hadn't found a single stick!

Then, through the swirling snow,
he saw a cave.
"It looks warm in there," he thought.
"Maybe there's a fire!" So he went inside . . .

There wasn't a fire, just a big, golden egg.
And it was HOT, hot water bottle hot!

Rupert picked the egg up, and felt its warmth
spread from his nose to his toes.
"Lovely," he sighed.

Then he thought of his poor mum and dad in their freezing cottage. He put the egg in his basket and hurried home.

"Look what I found!" said Rupert.
"What is it?" asked Mum.
"WARM!" said Dad, and smiled for the first time that week!
But just then . . .

Tap!

Tap!

CRACK!

. . . out hatched a **baby fire dragon!**

"Wow!" said Rupert.
"Ooh!" said Mum.
"No, no, NO!" cried Dad. "NO dragons!
They're nothing but trouble! You'll have to take
it back RIGHT NOW!"

The baby dragon blinked and sniffled.
His bottom lip wobbled and he
began to cry.

"Hush," said Rupert. "Don't cry."
And he gave the little dragon
a BIG hug.

"Ooh! He's as warm as
toasted crumpets," gasped
Rupert. "You try, Mum."

So Mum hugged the dragon. Even Dad hugged the dragon.
"Can we keep him, Dad?" asked Rupert.
"We can call him Crumpet!"

All through the winter, Crumpet the dragon kept the family warm and snug.

He **dried** the washing.

He **warmed** the beds.

He even **made the toast!**

But the **hugs** were the **best!**
And everywhere that Rupert
went, Crumpet went too . . .

. . . except on **bath night**. Rupert **hated** bath night. The water was always cold and Mum made him wash behind his ears where his favourite dirt was.

Crumpet was **scared** of water, so he hid behind the sofa making worried squeaky noises till Rupert was dry and the water had gone.

Then he **hugged** him until he was
warm and toasty.

Soon, winter turned to spring.

The snow started to melt.

Flowers bloomed, and Crumpet started **to grow.**

And as he grew, he got . . .

HOTTER!

"It's boiling in here," groaned Dad.

"GO AWAY, CRUMPET!"

Crumpet went over to Mum for a hug. "OUCH!" yelled Mum. "You're too HOT to hug!"

Rupert hugged Crumpet, but it wasn't warm and snuggly any more. It was all hot and scorchy.

Then one day, Crumpet burned the toast, scorched the washing and set fire to Mum's best bedspread.

"THAT'S IT!"
shouted Mum and Dad.
"CRUMPET HAS
GOT TO GO!"

Early next morning, Rupert and Crumpet set off up the mountain. By now Crumpet was so hot that his feet left little scorchy footprints in the grass.

Even through his glove, Rupert's fingers felt horribly hot as Crumpet clung to his hand.

Then as they reached the bridge, Crumpet saw the water and gripped Rupert's hand even **tighter.**

"OWWWWWWW!"

Crumpet slipped backwards and fell **into the water**,

WHEE,

PLOP,

HISS!

"CRUMPET!" yelled Rupert, but Crumpet had disappeared in a cloud of steam.

Rupert jumped in to save him from the cold, mountain river . . .

But the water **wasn't** cold, it was lovely and **warm!** And there was Crumpet, splashing and gurgling and giggling.

Rupert hugged him tight. And it wasn't hot and scorchy
any more, it was toasted crumpety warm again.
The cold water had cooled Crumpet down!
  "That's better," said Rupert. "Let's go home."

And from that day on, Crumpet the dragon lived
happily with Rupert and his family. And now
whenever Crumpet gets too hot to hug . . .

...he has a great, big, **bubbly bath!**

Other hot stories
from Little Tiger Press